my first coloring book

ABOUT THIS BOOK

This beautiful book uses coloring activities to teach letters, numbers, colors, and shapes.

At the start of the book, there is only a small part of each picture to color. Working through the pages, there is gradually more and more for children to complete as they master the skills.

make believe ideas

A
apples

Color the leaves on the apples!

How many apples can you see?

2

B
bee

Color the bee's stripes.

Color the cat's spots!

cat

D
dog

Draw the missing leash and color the dog's ear.

How many bone treats can you see?

E

elephant

Color the
elephant's
balancing ball!

6

Color a beautiful hat for the fish.

fish

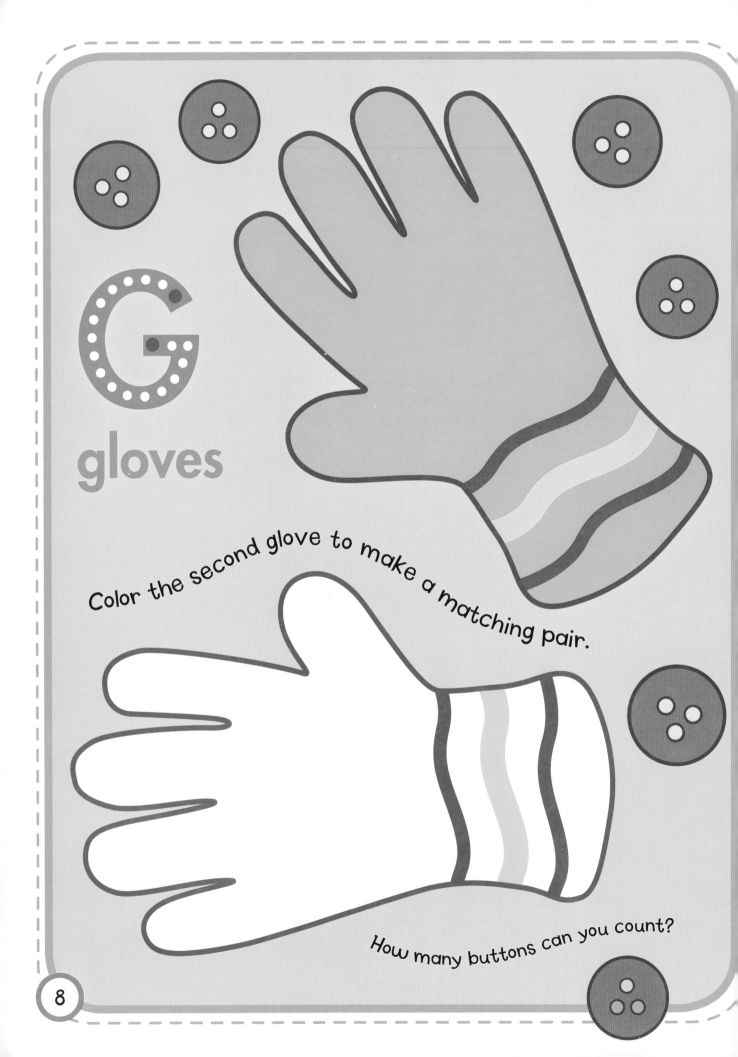

G

gloves

Color the second glove to make a matching pair.

How many buttons can you count?

8

H
house

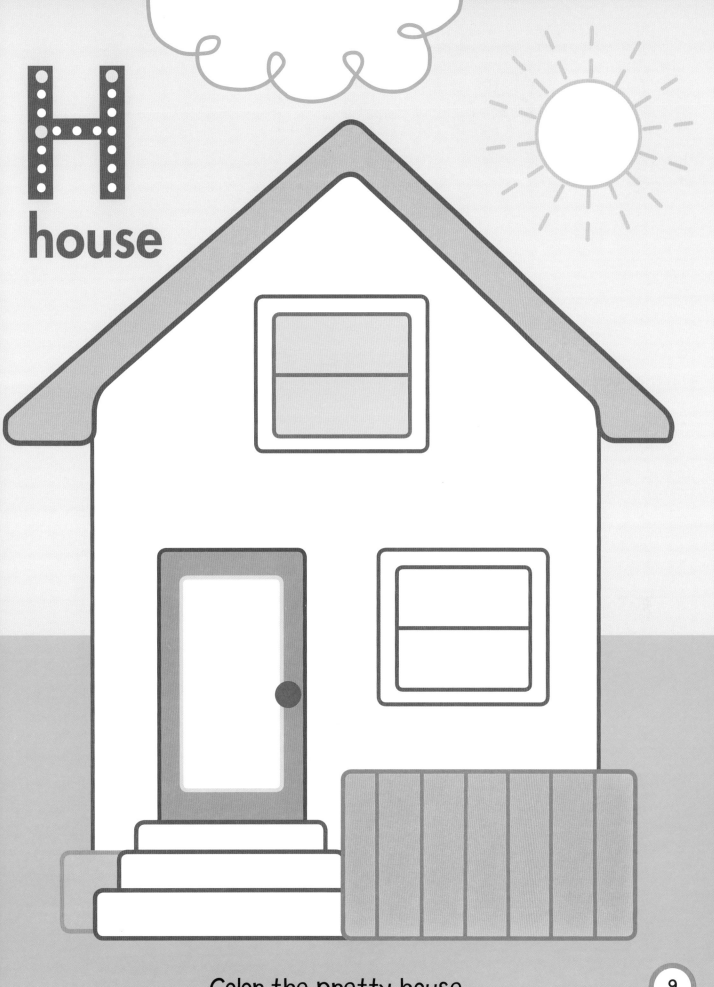

Color the pretty house.

9

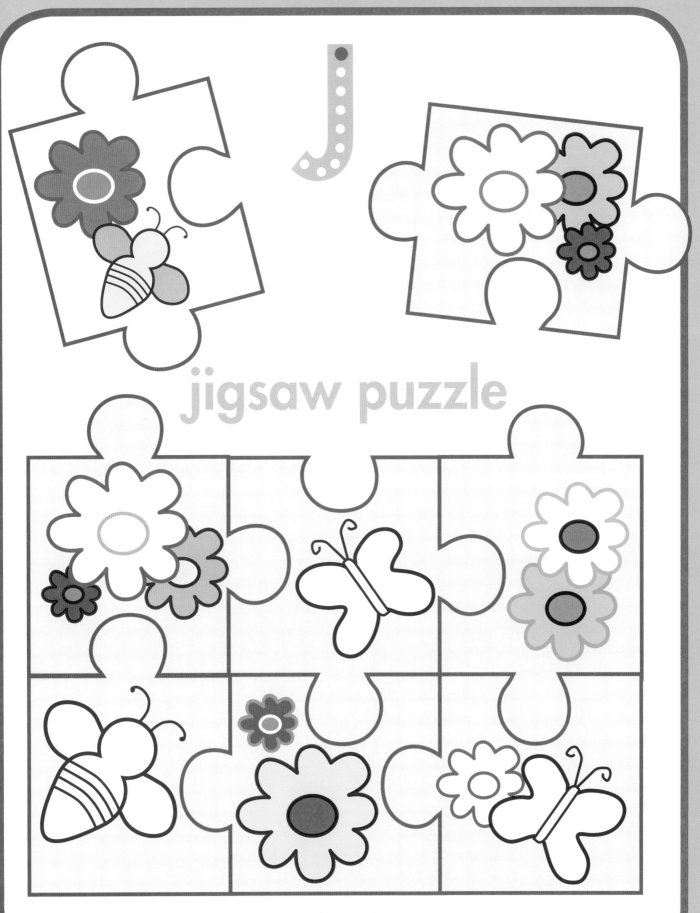

jigsaw puzzle

Color the butterflies, flowers, and bee.

K

kite

Color the patterns on the kite.

How many ribbons can you see on the kite's tail?

L

Color the ladybug on the flower.

Draw the missing petals, then color the flower.

ladybugs

13

M

mouse

Color the little mouse.

Give the mouse
a curly tail.

14

N

Color the eggs in the nest at night.

nest

15

O oranges

Color a juicy orange.

Who's that munching on the leaf?

16

Color the pirate's hat and coins.

How many coins can you count?

pirate

Q

queen

Color the queen's beautiful crown.

R

rabbit

Color the bouncing rabbit.

What do rabbits love to eat?

19

S

snail

Color the snail's spotted shell.

T treasure

Color the
treasure!

21

V van

Color the van on a
hot summer's day.

Draw the bumpy road.

W

whale

Color the whale
splashing in the sea.

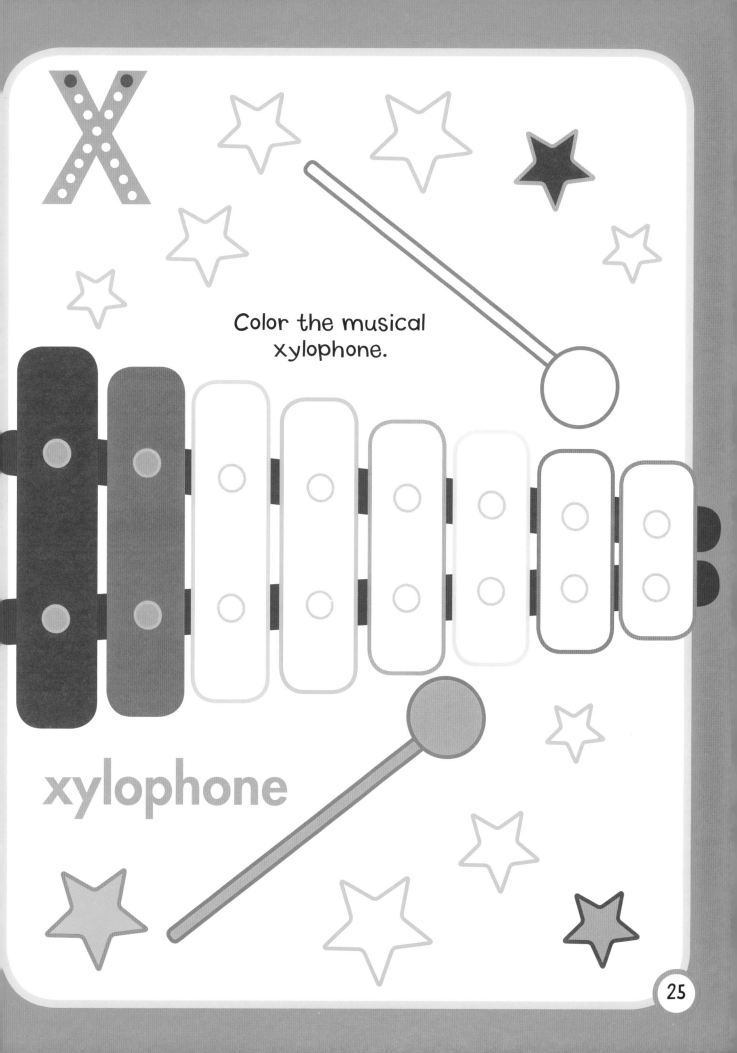

Color the musical xylophone.

xylophone

25

Y

yolk

Color the splats of egg yolk!

26

Z zebra

Color the zebra's stripes.

How many flowers can you count?

27

Color one happy clown.

28

2

Color two munching dinosaurs.

Color three
bears with
yummy cupcakes.

4

Color four
sailboats
at sea.

Draw the sails.

Color five rockets exploring space.

6

Color **six** delicious pieces of fruit.

How many seeds can you count in the melon?

7

Color seven jars filled with sweet treats.

Where did the ladybug find the lollipop?

8

The octopus has **eight** legs. Make each leg a different color.

What has the octopus found?

9

Color nine busy bugs.

Draw patterns on the butterfly's wings.

10

Color ten fish!

How many shells can you count?

Color this present bright yellow.

Color the spotted present blue.

Color the striped present green.

Color presents for the cat and mouse. Use the colors shown.

42

Color this present orange.

Color this present red.

Color this present purple.

The gray mouse wants to put his cheese in the pink present.

43

Color the tractor red.

44

Color the flag green with orange stars.

Color the big elephant to match the little elephant.

Color the pink custard the elephants are squirting.

46

Color the cow brown with orange patches.

Make the happy dinosaur bright and colorful!

Draw the moon at night and color the two birds.

Color the train red, blue, and yellow!

How many butterflies can you count?

Make Teddy and his plane your favorite colors.

Fill the happy ice-cream bars with rainbow colors.

Which ice-cream bar is melting?

Color the rabbits in blue, red, and purple.

Draw the rabbit's bouncing yo-yo

54

The spiders are hiding. How many can you see?

Make the alien's spaceship bright and colorful.

Make the chicks
different colors.

Draw the chick's cracked shell.

57

Color the desserts to make them look delicious.

Who's nibbling the donuts?

Color the happy submarine
and all his treasure.

a brown oval

a gray semi-circle

Make all the shapes the right color.

an orange square

a pink star

a green triangle

a yellow diamond

a red circle

a purple rectangle

a blue heart

Finish coloring the dog's house of shapes.

What shaped snacks is the dog eating?

Color the starfish twins and all of their star friends.

What is different about this twin?

Color the butterfly made of circles.

66

Color the boat made of triangles.

Color the shark fins in the sea.

67

Color the
shape robot.

How many triangles
can you find?

Color the curly sheep. He has oval ears.

What do sheep like to eat?

Color the amazing-shaped birds.

Can you find two heart shapes?

Color the snake full of shapes.

72

Color the lion under a starry night sky.

Color the fun forest of shapes.

74

How many ladybugs can you find?

Color all the shapes in space.

76

Color the square boxes in the basement.

What's hiding in this box?

Draw this box.

Color a house
made of shapes.

How many
different shapes
can you find?

Color the ice-cream treat!